Tristan and Iseult, the most famous pair of lovers in Logres.

Sir Clutterbuck, a little-known knight who lumbered through the Dark Ages, snoring loudly.

and fearsome beast.

Nimue, a Maiden of the Lake, and a good friend to Merlin.

Sir Galahad, the whitest, purest and most faultless knight.

Sir Perceval, a young kitten who grew up in the forest.

Sir Bedivere, whose task was to cast Excalibur back into the Lake from whence it came.

The Grail, a strange decorated cream-jug that turned the heads and whiskers of the Knights of the Round Table.

Lady Lynette, a damsel in distress.

Sir Bors, one of Arthur's most loyal knights.

The Red Knight, who decorated a tree with a couple of dozen knights.

The Witch Pigmalion, who was rescued by Sir Lancelot.

LOGRES

This sceptred isle of cats, and King Arthur's kingdom.

Sir Pellinore's castle

The castle of the Brothers of Orkney – Gawain, Gareth Beaumains, Agravain, and Gaheris (and Mordred, too)

The castle of Morgan le Fay and King Urien

Sir Lancelot's castle, where Guinevere escaped to

Iseult's home, before all the troubles with Mark and Tristan

Sir Paul's manor and estates (and studio)

Perceval's forest, where he grew up

The wall marking the northern borders of the ancient Lion Kingdom

The castle of Sir Hector and his son Sir Kay, where Arthur spent his kittenhood

Lyonesse's castle

King Leo's castle, where the Round Table was kept before it was removed to Catmelot

The Isle of Avalon, a rest-home for distinguished cats

Tintagel, birthplace of Arthur and the castle of Uther Pendragon

The Dancing Giants that Merlin marched over to Logres with his magic powers

King Mark's castle

Tristan's Stone

Catmelot, Arthur's castle and court

The castle of Sir Clutterbuck (please do not disturb)

Sir Tristan's castle

Sir Galahad's castle

The Spooky Chapel

FOREWORD

Some years ago, I produced a book entitled *The Canine Kalevala*. In this volume dogs were given a chance to tell of their glorious past before the days of leash and collar. The response was mostly positive. On my morning walks I have noticed a marked lessening of angry yapping, barking and bared teeth in my direction, and indeed on one or two occasions dogs have actually licked my hand.

Our own domestic animal, however, is a cat – who goes by the name of Kille. I have understood from a normally well-informed source that the scratching of our carpets and armchairs will not cease before a similar book, or preferably a better one, is published about cats.
 I must nevertheless state immediately that despite many attempts I have found it more difficult to penetrate the minds of cats than of dogs. Hence I am taking a far, far greater risk in presenting this book. On the other hand, in my view the stories of King Arthur and the Knights of the Round Table are even better known internationally than the tales of Finland's *Kalevala*. In this respect, at least, I hope and assume they will satisfy our own Kille and the other cats in the neighbourhood.

But I guess the barking will start up again now.

Espoo, 7.5.1997

Mauri Kunnas

For Kille Kitten, Noora
and Jenna, and of course
for Sir Paul as well

Translated from the abridged Finnish version
by William Moore

Illustration and text © Doghill Productions Oy
The original title *Kuningas Artturin ritarit* published
by Otava Publishing Company Ltd 1997
English translation © Wordcraft Ky

Printed by:
Otava Book Printing Ltd
Keuruu 1999

ISBN 951-1-15377-3

THE TAILS OF
KING ARTHUR

AND THE KNIGHTS OF THE ROUND TABLE

A CHAPTER OF EARLY FELINE HISTORY

MAURI KUNNAS
TARJA KUNNAS

OTAVA PUBLISHING COMPANY LTD, HELSINKI

THE SWORD IN THE STONE

Long ago, cats lived in their own island kingdom, Logres by name. The cats had great kings to rule them. They were noble and fair in their dealings, not just to cats, but also to dogs, pigs, even to mice.

But before long the news of the fine island over the sea came to the ears of the beach-rats and the seawolves. They wanted to take the cats' island for themselves.

In those days, the King of the Cats was Uther Pendragon. It was a good thing that Uther was a strong fellow, for he had to fight constantly with the seawolves. Luckily his best friend was Merlin, the most powerful wizard and magician in all of Logres. Together they kept the intruders at bay.

Tales told that Merlin was the son of an elf-king and a forest princess.

Cats didn't know much about elves, except that they were a pretty scary bunch, and it was best not to upset them.

4

Uther and Queen Igraine had long hoped for a son who would become king after Uther.

At last, one Christmas night a little tom-kitten was born, who took the name Arthur.

"Arthur will grow to be a great king. He will restore order to the Isle of the Cats", said Merlin. "He will become a great and respected ruler."

"Huh? Why Arthur and not me?" grumbled Morgan, Arthur's sister. But in those days a girl could not become king.

Soon the seawolves were attacking Logres again. "The kitten must be taken to safety", ordered Merlin, and one dark winter's night he galloped away, carrying a bundle that made feeble mewing noises.

Nobody knew where Merlin had taken Arthur, except of course Igraine, who often went secretly to see how her son was getting on.

Merlin took Arthur to the castle of his friend Sir Hector, a tough old tomcat.

"Whose kitten is it, then?" asked Sir Hector when they arrived at the castle, deep in the forest. But Merlin would not say.

"You will be told, when the time is right", muttered Merlin. "Just bring him up to be a good and fair-minded knight."

Sir Hector had a kitten of his own, named Kay. Arthur and Kay became firm friends.

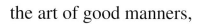

Sir Hector taught the two lads all the knightly skills: bravery, gentleness, swordsmanship and riding,

the art of good manners,

how to handle hawks for hunting,

and of course, reading and sums.

But in their spare time, the two would-be knights liked best to go hunting for dragons' nests. And Sir Hector often had to smear grease on the boys' scorched tails after another close call with a fiery dragon.

Uther Pendragon ruled Logres for many years, but in time he grew weary of all that fighting.

"I've had enough", Uther grunted, after a particularly nasty scuffle with the beach-rats. "Someone else can take over. Cats only have nine lives, you know."

And so Uther went off to Avalon, to the island where all brave cat-warriors retire to lick their wounds in the evening of their lives.

Merlin called the knights and the other nobles together in an old abbey. "It is time to select a new High King", thundered the magician.

The noble cats growled and looked sideways at each other. Things did *not* look good – everyone wanted to be the new ruler.

And then a miracle happened.

In the churchyard there had appeared a great stone and on it an anvil, and thrust deep into it was a sword. Everyone rushed outside. Merlin read the text on the stone: "He that can pull the sword from the anvil shall be the new High King of Logres!"

All the knights pushed and shoved so that they could be the first to grab the sword.

"Wait your turn, wait your turn!" bellowed Merlin. But however hard they each tugged, the sword would not move the tiniest bit.

"On New Year's Day we shall arrange a tournament, to which we shall invite all the knights in the realm", declared Merlin. "Fear not, we shall find a new High King!"

He that pulleth the sworde from yon anvyle shalle be the new

The invitation to the tournament also went to Sir Hector and his two boys. Kay had just been made a knight, and Arthur was his squire, carrying his sword and armour.

Outside the tournament ground, Arthur noticed that Sir Kay's sword had disappeared.

"Some squire you are", snapped Sir Hector. "Find that sword, on the double!"

Arthur looked high and low, but Sir Kay's sword was nowhere to be found. Finally, he stumbled into a churchyard, and he saw a sword stuck deep into a stone anvil. It was a strange place to keep it, but the sword looked just fine.

"I suppose this will do for Kay", thought Arthur, and he pulled the sword from the stone.

Arthur was made to put the sword back into the anvil and pull it out again, and again, and again, before the astonished Sir Hector finally believed his eyes.

"Well, I'll be a cross-eyed tabby tom... this boy's the King!"

Word of what had happened spread in a flash, and everyone flocked to the churchyard.

"What? That? That's supposed to be the King?" hissed the noble cats when they saw Arthur. "But he's only a beardless kitten!"

And then Merlin stepped forward, and revealed Arthur's secret.

"Long live King Arthur!" shouted Sir Kay, and pretty soon all the others took up the cry.

Old Sir Hector got a terrible fright – he knew the famous sword immediately.

"What have you two kitlings done now?" he spluttered.

"Don't be angry, Uncle!" whined Arthur. "I'll stick it straight back in the stone."

And they all marched off to the churchyard.

At Candlemas, a month later, Arthur was crowned King of Logres.
He was given a shiny shield and a splendid horned helmet, the ancient
symbols of the old Cat Kings of Logres, carried by his father before him.
   "Be always fair, brave and fearless, and walk tall with your shield and
helmet", ordered Merlin sternly. "For you are now High King of all the Cats!"
   "Phooey!" muttered Morgan, Arthur's sister, standing behind the crowd.

The dukes and earls and princes
of Logres gave Arthur many fine
presents. The one he liked most,
however, was from Sir Kay – a
bright red dragon pup called
Cabal.

"I don't expect I'll be able to
do much hunting for
dragons' nests anymore",
Arthur thought to himself.

SIR PELLINORE AND EXCALIBUR

Arthur moved to the splendid castle of Catmelot. Sir Kay took charge of the Royal Treasury, and Merlin became the King's special adviser. If anyone needed advice, Arthur did.

The young king would have loved to join the other knights having adventures, but Merlin wouldn't let him.

"That sort of nonsense isn't for you", he said. "Remember a king's most important weapon is not his sword, but good sense and fairmindedness."

One day, Sir Kay returned puffing and wheezing from his morning run.

"My Lord", he panted. "There's a strange knight out there. I told him to be on his way, but he just tied my tail in a knot!"

"Aaa-Ha!" cried Arthur. "Bring my shield and helmet! This adventure belongs to me!"

In the forest, Arthur saw a most
curious sight.

A very angry-looking tom was
shaking the trunk of a large tree.
In the branches was perched the
oddest monster, making barking
noises.

"What is THAT?" said Arthur.
"And who, Sir, are you?"

"Sir Pellinore is my name",
replied the grumpy knight.
"But keep your puny whiskers
out of this! Ten years I've chased
this beast, and now I've got him.
Go home, milksop. I've no time
to play with kittens."

Before Merlin could stop him,
Arthur charged at the knight,
waving his lance before him.

But the wily knight dodged, and
Arthur crashed into the tree. The
monster fell slap onto the necks of
Arthur and Pellinore and went off
barking into the forest.

"You dunderhead!" roared the
knight. "You'll pay for this!"

Arthur ran off as fast as his paws
could carry him.

Fortunately Merlin was close by, and
with a few magic words he charmed Sir
Pellinore into a deep and dreamless
sleep where he sat.

"Well, you're not short of bravery", laughed Merlin, "but you need to learn to use your head first."

"But how was I to know that the big oaf would get so bent out of shape?" wailed Arthur. "A-and my sword's broken. Now Kay will laugh at me."

"It's time you had a new sword", said Merlin mysteriously. "But you must be worthy of it."

Merlin took Arthur to a shimmering lake.
  "This is the Lake of Reeds, a lake of much power", he whispered. "Here you shall get your sword."
  And just then a hand appeared from the water, bearing a glittering sword.

A golden-haired maiden approached them across the misty water. "She is Nimue, the Maiden of the Lake", murmured Merlin.
  "So you are the noble King Arthur", said the maiden. "Merlin has spoken highly of you."
  A boat floated into view from the reeds.

"Go, fetch your sword!" said Nimue, and Arthur stepped into the boat, his knees trembling. He took the glittering sword, and a fine scabbard to sheathe it in.

"It is Excalibur, it has magical powers", explained Nimue. "The sword will bring you victory, and the scabbard will heal your wounds."

Arthur promised to use the sword well, to bring fortune to the entire Kingdom of the Cats.

On their way home, Merlin made Arthur invisible, as he had to wake Sir Pellinore.

"That darned cub!" snarled the knight.

"That darned cub is also High King, you know", chuckled Merlin.

Sir Pellinore went rather pale.

"Don't worry", said the magician. "The King invites brave knights like you to his Round Table in Catmelot."

"D-Do I?" stuttered Arthur a moment later. "And WHAT Round Table?"

GUINEVERE AND THE ROUND TABLE

In time, Arthur became a good and wise king. All the bravest knights in Logres arrived at Catmelot, as they all wanted to ride alongside him.

One day a messenger arrived: Bad news! A bandit baron had surrounded King Leodegrance's castle.

"Let's move!" shouted Merlin. "Leo is an old dear friend, and if I recall, he also has a pretty daughter, Guinevere."

The knights were ready to ride immediately, even though King Leo was a dog.

Bullying barons usually ran off as soon as they heard the hoof-beats of Arthur and his knights, and that's just what happened here.

Leo didn't know how he could thank Arthur.

"I've no gold, but you can have my round table. It's in good shape, if you don't mind a few holes. Guinevere uses it as a dartboard, you see."

Merlin frowned.

"Ah, the Round Table!" remembered Arthur.

Merlin had crafted the table long ago, and stories said the wizard's magic had gone into the making of it.

Arthur stayed many days as Leo's guest. He felt that young Guinevere was such good company, even if she WAS a dog, that he had no great wish to go home at all.

"What if I were to come home with you?" she asked him.

Arthur was delighted.

"On one condition", said Guinevere. "I want to be Queen!"

And that's just what happened.

A splendid royal wedding was held at Catmelot. Everybody cheered: "Long live Arthur and Guinevere!" They danced and sang, what a din there was! "Time for the darts competition!" shouted Guinevere. "Stand the round table on its side!"

In a few moments, the darts were flying.

"Yippee! Catspaw!" yelled Arthur.

Merlin had retired to the castle tower for a nap, but the noise woke him. He hurried down to the great hall.

"Get that table down, IMMEDIATELY", he roared. "It has secret powers you know nothing of!"

When Merlin had cooled off and order was restored, something very strange happened.

The names of the knights appeared on the table, and on the backs of the chairs around it.

At least on all the chairs save one, which read "SIEGE PERILOUS".

Siege Perilous

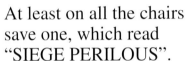

Merlin pointed to the chair and declared: "This is reserved for a knight as white as the driven snow, as blue as the midsummer sky, and golden like the Sun. When he arrives, the knights will leave the Round Table, and the last days of Logres will be upon us. But that day is many years hence."

"Pish!" muttered Sir Kay. "No such thing as a golden cat." And he sat down in the forbidden chair. Luckily there was a tub of cold cream nearby, because the chair scorched the fur off poor Kay's backside.

The knights swore an oath, the oath of the Round Table. They promised to keep out of all mischief, to help those weaker than themselves, and to protect damsels in distress.

"And promise me there will be NO more nonsense with this table", growled Merlin, glaring at the knights and at Queen Guinevere in particular.

The knights nodded and promised to keep their oath. Guinevere promised, too, even though she was not a knight, or even a cat.

And that was the beginning of the story of the Feline Knights of the Round Table.

Arthur's knights criss-crossed the country on their adventures, knocking bullies out of their saddles and rescuing damsels in distress.

The keenest of them all was Sir Lancelot of the Lake. All the prettiest kitties of Logres admired him, although Sir Kay said that he looked more like a frog than a real cat.

Lancelot was especially loyal in his services to Guinevere, Arthur's queen.

The noble knight would grant her every wish, whether she asked him to pick some wild flowers or send pesky dragons on their way.

But Lancelot always found time to help the other ladies of the court, too.

The witches of Logres thought that Arthur's knights were silly oafs with buckets on their heads, and they loved to play tricks on them.

Once upon a time, Lancelot met a maiden dressing the wounds of an injured knight.

"Sir Lancelot", she begged. "Please help us. My brother was preparing to fight Sir Wriggly, but suddenly his nose began to bleed."

"This is the work of that nasty Witch Pigmalion", wailed the maiden. "She said the bleeding will not stop until a brave knight enters the Spooky Chapel at midnight and cuts a piece from the skeleton's cloak, to wipe my brother's nose."

"In the name of the Queen, I shall do my best, fair maiden", promised Lancelot.

Lancelot came to the Spooky Chapel. Now he was as brave as any knight, but he was awfully afraid of the bogeyman. Inside was a skeleton on a stone tomb. With his paws knocking together, Lancelot cut off a piece of the scarlet cloak, and tiptoed out.

Just as he thought it was all over, he saw an enormous skeleton, dangling in the wind. It wasn't *really* a skeleton, but a wooden puppet that Witch Pigmalion had put together.

"Booo-aaahh", cackled Pigmalion, and pulled on the strings, so the huge skeleton began to dance and wave its arms.

Lancelot turned and ran, and so he didn't see the strings break and the skeleton come tumbling down on top of that wicked Pigmalion.

The witch was all tangled in the strings of her puppet, and she fell over onto an ants' nest. "Help, Helppp!" she squealed. The ants didn't like being disturbed.

The gallant Lancelot immediately ran back. Luckily for him, the monster had disappeared.

"At your service, pretty maid", he puffed, and helped to free the witch.

"Pretty maid? Who? Me?" giggled the blushing Pigmalion. "Thank you kindly, my brave knight."

When Lancelot returned, the wounded knight's nose had stopped bleeding. A piece of wool tied to his tail had fixed it.

"It's an old trick of my mum's", said Sir Wriggly, and he invited the knight and his sister home to eat pancakes. It was more fun than sword-fighting, anyway.

Witch Pigmalion never troubled the Knights again. In fact she told all the other witches how a noble knight had rescued her, a fair maiden in distress, from a giant skeleton and the teeth of a thousand beady-eyed little monsters.

"Must have been a dark and stormy night – or that Lanceclod is as blind as a bat", chuckled the other witches.

THE KNIGHT OF THE GREASY SPOON

One morning, a tattered tom-kitten arrived in Catmelot.

"My Lord Arthur!" said he. "I beg three things of you, my King."

"Well, let's hear them", replied Arthur.

"First, I wish to come to live in Catmelot."

"Really?" Arthur was interested now. "And the other two wishes?"

"Later, Sire, a year from now", said the youngster.

Sir Kay snorted: "Cheeky little rascal!"

"Now, now, Sir Kay", laughed Arthur. "Let the boy stay and work in the castle."

"Well, if you wash up and help the cook, you can sleep under the kitchen table", promised Sir Kay grudgingly.

And this was fine with the youngster.

But the kitten was so clumsy that Sir Kay dubbed him Greasy Spoon.

The lad was always dropping soup bowls and burning the porridge. Arthur's cook lost his temper, and he left and never came back.

This left Greasy Spoon in charge of all the Catmelot cooking...

That year Arthur's knights did even more adventuring, since everyone wanted to be as far from the Catmelot kitchens as possible at dinner-time.

Soon there was nobody left in the castle but Arthur and Sir Kay.

A year passed, and then one day, in burst a fair maiden in a lot of distress.

"My name is Lynette", she wept. "The Red Knight is besieging the castle of my sister

Lyonesse. His mean brothers, the Green and Black Knights, are skulking out there somewhere nearby. Please, Sire, send one of your brave knights to free my sister."

Just then, in rushed Greasy Spoon from the kitchen.

"Sire! It is time for my two other requests. First, grant this adventure to me, and if I succeed, make me a knight on my return."

Sir Kay sniggered: "Hah! Plan to knock them out with a soup-spoon, laddie?"

"Hmm... why not?" grinned the lad, and ran off to the kitchen to fetch some tools.

"You shall have your adventure!" laughed Arthur.

The Lady Lynette made a rude face.

"Hah!" she hissed. "No thanks! I'd sooner fight them myself!"

But the kitchen boy left with her
all the same.

"Stay back!" she grumbled.
"You smell of onions!"

They met the Black Knight in
the forest.

"Halt, my lady! Is *this* your brave champion?"
he sneered.

"He's not a knight", Lady Lynette spluttered.
"Just an undercook from the kitchens."

"A pot-rattling boy to defend a noble lady?" roared
the knight, and charged towards Greasy Spoon.

In a flash, Greasy Spoon tossed some black pepper
through the visor of the Black Knight's helmet.

"Black pepper for a Black Knight", chuckled the lad.

"Aaaaa-CHOO! Ah-CHOOOO!" bellowed the knight,
and he fell out of his saddle onto the ground. Thump!

Soon Greasy Spoon and Lynette met the Green Knight.

"Ho there, fair lady! Is this scruffy fur-ball to protect
your sister?" he enquired.

"Him? Nah... he's just a pesky pot-boy who follows
me", said the maid dismissively.

"Then I'll send him back to his pots!" shouted
the knight, and galloped towards Greasy Spoon.

"Green beans for a Green
Knight!" cried the kitten, and
tossed a handful of beans
under the horse's hooves.

The horse fell over in a heap.
And that was the end of the
Green Knight.

Finally the pair arrived at Lady Lyonesse's castle. The Red Knight had hung twenty knightly cats by their tails from the branches of an oak tree.

But Greasy Spoon wasn't at all worried by this.

"Ha! No wonder Catmelot's been so empty!" he laughed, and he blew hard on a large horn that was hanging from the tree.

The Red Knight looked out from his tent.

"More decorations for my tree!" chuckled the knight, and he rushed outside, putting on his helmet.

The two braves charged towards each other. Then Greasy Spoon reached into his bag and took out a jar of jam.

"Red jam for a Red Knight!" he crowed, and splatted the contents of the jar right inside the Red Knight's helmet.

"Help! I can't see a thing!" whined the Red Knight, and rode straight into the castle moat.

And so the Lady Lyonesse and the twenty dangling knights were freed, and Greasy Spoon became a hero.

"Let's feed the Red Knight a pot of Greasy Spoon's fish soup as a punishment", said Sir Gawain. "How's that sound, Greasy Spoon?"

"Fine, but only if my brothers here give me a hand", replied the young hero.

The knights looked astonished.

Did Greasy Spoon have brothers?

"Gawain, Gaheris, Agravain – do you still not know me?" asked Greasy Spoon. "I am Gareth of Orkney, your little brother."

"Gareth!? You were only an unweaned kitten when we left home", said an astonished Gawain.

"I was. And when I wanted to join you, you said there was no room on the trip for a mewling kitten-cub", laughed Greasy Spoon.

The fish soup was three times worse than normal. The Red Knight got his punishment.

Of course Lady Lynette married her champion, Greasy Spoon. And Sir Gareth Beaumains, Knight of the Greasy Spoon – well, he never learnt to cook, but he *was* good at washing dishes.

MORGAN LE FAY

Morgan le Fay was Arthur's sister, and she also had magic powers.

"That bro of mine was born with a silver cream spoon in his mouth", she grumbled. "Somebody should teach him a lesson, or his head's going to get too big for his whiskers."

One day, Morgan and her husband Urien, King of Gore, were visiting Arthur and Guinevere in Catmelot.

"Morgan is up to something, Arthur", warned Merlin. "Look out."

"Oh fiddlesticks, Merlin, you worrypot", laughed Arthur.

Arthur, Urien and their friend Sir Accolon had decided to go fishing. They stayed too long and it got dark.

Suddenly they saw a beautiful boat, all lit up, carrying nine lovely maidens.

"Climb aboard, gentle knights!" crooned the maidens.

The anglers hopped into the boat, and the maidens brought them delicious dishes, and some wonderful sweet honeyed milk.

Our heroes were so busy drinking, they didn't notice that one of the maidens looked familiar.

The milk was mixed with some special magic herbs, and suddenly all three dropped into a deep sleep.

In the morning, King Urien woke up
in the guest room at Catmelot.

Arthur wasn't so lucky. He woke up
in a pitch-dark dungeon.

A dusky maiden appeared at the door.
"Noble Sir", she said. "If you will fight
against the wicked Sir Curmudgeon,
you will be freed."

"Certainly, madam", replied Arthur,
but he noticed that his sword Excalibur
was missing.

The maiden handed Arthur another sword.
"Hmph!" muttered the king.
"Am I supposed to make do with this?"

Meanwhile, Sir Accalon was being hoisted
from a well.

"The noble Morgan le Fay begs you to
fight against the wicked Sir Curmudgeon",
wheezed a beady-eyed fellow, "and guess
what, you can use the King's sword,
Excalibur."

Dressed in strange clothes, Arthur and Accolon did not recognise each other. Each thought the other was Sir Curmudgeon.

Arthur was immediately in trouble.

"Ouch! He's got Excalibur!" he squealed. "I haven't got a chance."

"The unbeatable Arthur!" giggled Morgan from the castle walls. "Not so proud now, eh?"

Luckily for Arthur, Merlin and Nimue were out picking flowers close by. They heard the noise and rushed over.

Now it was Arthur's turn to give his opponent a good thrashing.

"Mercy! You win!" cried Accolon.

Arthur recognised his friend's voice. "Accolon? This is one of Morgan's schemes!"

"Ahem. What did I tell you?" said Merlin drily.

On their way back to Catmelot, Arthur and Sir Accolon spent the night in a monastery.
But Morgan had followed them.

"I'm going to pinch your magic sword!" hissed Morgan.
At midnight, Morgan crept into Arthur's bed-chamber.
But Arthur always kept Excalibur under his pillow.
Still, all the rest of Arthur's equipment was there by the bed.
"Hmph. I'll take these then. You won't be able to brag about your toys anymore."
A rattling noise woke Arthur up.

"Robbers! After them!" cried the King, and stumbled outside.

Three horses were soon galloping headlong in the moonlight. Morgan and her little helper rushed by, with Arthur and Sir Accolon in hot pursuit.

"They're catching us!" cackled the beady-eyed one. "Toss that junk into the river!"
And so Uther Pendragon's shield and helmet went into the stream, along with Arthur's magic scabbard.

Morgan cast a spell to turn herself and her
assistant into a rock.
"Where did they disappear to?"
puzzled Arthur.

The King returned to Catmelot feeling very down in the dumps. But then Morgan le Fay herself appeared.

"I hope you aren't angry, brother dear, even if your trinkets did fall into that river", miaowed Morgan. "It was a complete accident, you know. Anyway, I've brought a magic cloak that will make you invincible in battle", she said sweetly. "Do try it on!"

"Morgan, why don't you wear it?", said Merlin softly.
   "Oh, no, it's far too big for me", protested Morgan, but in the end she had to put on the cloak.

Morgan jumped high into the air. "Ack! Owww!" she screeched. "Get it off me! Those fleas are biting me!"
   And waving her flea-ridden cloak, Morgan swept out of the room.
   "Oh, those tricks of my sis", sighed Arthur.
   But after that, Morgan never caused her brother any more trouble.

TRISTAN AND ISEULT

One of Arthur's knights was called Sir Tristan. He was very good with a sword, but he was also the most famous bard in Logres, singing and playing the harp.

Now Sir Tristan had an uncle, King Mark.

"Sing to me, Tristan. Lighten my heavy heart with a song", begged King Mark.

King Mark was feeling very low because his cabbageball team had played against the team of his neighbour King Anguisel, and lost 8–0.

And now Anguisel wanted a sword-fighting contest between the two kingdoms.

"Anguisel has Marhaus, a tough heavyweight tomcat", wailed Mark. "I don't have any knights to match him."

"Let me go, then", said Tristan.

And so Tristan went off to the big fight.

It was a bruising contest, but in the end Tristan won. Marhaus slunk back home to lick his wounds.

A piece of Tristan's sword had broken off, and was sticking out of Marhaus's head. Anguisel's pretty daughter Iseult got it out.

"Stupid tomcat games", muttered Iseult, and she popped the bit of sword into her jewel-case.

King Mark had another reason for being sad. He had no queen.

Mark had heard about his rival Anguisel's pretty daughter Iseult, and he wanted her for his wife.

"I know", thought Mark. "I'll send Tristan to woo her for me. It's hard to resist a song from a chap like Tristan."

The ever-helpful Sir Tristan sailed over the sea to Anguisel's castle.

When he arrived as an ambassador for King Mark, Tristan got a chilly reception, until he picked up his harp and broke into a song. Soon Tristan was the darling of the whole castle.

Even King Anguisel was won over by the lad's songs.

"Tristan, I'd like to reward you", said the king. "Ask for anything, and it's yours."

"Then grant me Iseult as a wife for my uncle King Mark", replied Sir Tristan.

Anguisel was not pleased. He'd have preferred Tristan as a son-in-law, but a promise was a promise.

Iseult didn't mind, though. She'd seen Tristan's sword and the missing piece. "Rather King Mark than some swashbuckler like that Sir Tristan", she muttered.

And so the king sent the youngsters on their way.

"My dear girl. Take this minted milk along", whispered one of Iseult's ladies-in-waiting. "Offer it to Mark, and have a sip yourself."

The jug contained a love-potion. Whoever tasted the milk would fall hopelessly in love with the first person he or she saw.

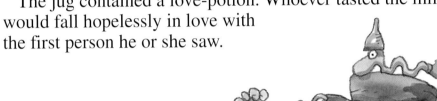

It was a hot day on the boat, and Tristan was sweating in his chain-mail on the deck. He found the strange jug of milk, took a swig, and passed it to the thirsty Iseult.

Pam! The potion worked immediately.

"Oh Thristhan, my handthome hero", lisped Iseult.

When the boat arrived, the lovers decided to elope together.

King Mark found nothing on it except a halfempty jug.

"Traitors!" he roared. He grabbed the jug and raced after them.

Mark was so angry he didn't look where he was going, and he ran slap into an old granny carrying some broomsticks.

"Whoops-a-daisy", said the old biddy.

Luckily the jug hadn't broken.

"Here, have a drink to revive yourself, handsome knight", she said, and she took a quick snort of milk herself.

And so King Mark and his new Queen lived happily ever after, making brooms in their castle.

Tristan and Iseult lived together at Catmelot. Sir Tristan was the greatest hero of the court, at least in his own songs. And Iseult thought so, too.

THE STORY OF LITTLE PERCEVAL

Sir Pellinore had a son, a kitten named Perceval. Pellinore wasn't home much – he was always out chasing that odd barking beast. Perceval's mother, Lady Goodheart, ran the whole castle by herself.

Finally, she'd had enough.

"I'll make sure Perceval doesn't turn out like that useless father of his", she muttered, and she and Perceval went to live deep in the forest. And so Perceval grew up with the flowers and the butterflies, and he didn't know a thing about King Arthur or his famous knights.

One day, however, he saw three noble, shiny creatures riding across the meadow.

"What were THEY, Mum?" he asked his mother.

"Um... they were angel-cats", she said hastily.

Lady Goodheart had resolved that her son would never hear a word about those pesky knights.

But from then on, Perceval always wanted to play "angel-cats".

One day Perceval galloped so far on his wooden horse that he arrived at Catmelot. He stood there, staring, at the door to the great hall. Just a few feet away were dozens of noisy angels, all tucking in to dinner.

As Perceval stared, a rude knight burst in on the party.
   "Ah, the nice lordycats slurping their cream", bellowed the knight. "How's about a swig for a bandit porker, eh?", and he snatched Guinevere's golden goblet and ran out of the door.

Before anyone knew what had happened, young Perceval had set off after the ugly outlaw knight.
   "Oy, you!" yelled Sir Kay. "Come back! This is an adventure for knights!"
   But the kitten was long gone.
   Perceval caught up with the robber when he stopped to admire his loot.

"Give that goblet back!" piped Perceval.
   "Wha..? They sent a little flea like you?" the ugly knight grunted. "Guess what I'll give you, laddie – a walloping!"
The knight charged towards little Perceval.
   But just then Perceval noticed an interesting shiny beetle on the ground, and he bent down to examine it.
   The horse thundered over Perceval, and the knight's lance thudded into the ground, catapulting its owner into the air.

Merlin had seen everything.

"That was bravely done!" he smiled. "Now, according to the knightly rules, your opponent's treasure and equipment are yours."

"Really?" Perceval's eyes opened wide. "And will I become a real angel, too?"

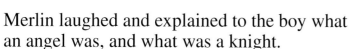

Merlin laughed and explained to the boy what an angel was, and what was a knight.

Perceval dragged all his shiny new things back to Catmelot.

"Nice gear", said Sir Kay, "but... where's the queen's goblet?"

"Oh, it's there somewhere, but don't you think this is *much* finer?" replied the boy, and he pulled out a gleaming silvery beetle.

Merlin carved Perceval some more suitable knightly equipment, a fine oak rocking horse and a sword. And Guinevere's drinking goblet made a fine helmet.

"Run along home now, your mother must be worried", ordered Merlin. "You can come and collect these things just as soon as your Mum says you are big enough to become a real knight."

(The silvery beetle, by the way, later became the famous Sir Paul, but that – as they say – is quite another story.)

MERLIN'S FAREWELL

The years went by and there was peace in Logres. The seawolves and beach-rats were driven over the sea.

The Knights of the Round Table had time for joisting at tournaments, saving damsels in distress every now and then, and for going off adventuring whenever they felt like it. Life was a bowl of cream, thank you very much.

As time passed, a few streaks of grey appeared on the fur of King Arthur and his knights.

"Are we starting to show our age?" laughed the knights.

Merlin was much older than any of the knights, and he suffered from gout.

"It comes from living in that cold, draughty castle", said his friend Nimue. "It's high time you retired to the comforts of the Isle of Avalon. Come on, dear, I'll take you there myself."

And so Merlin left Catmelot.

He spoke to Arthur and the knights: "From now on, you're on your own. Look after the Table, and remember your oath!"

And then he was gone.

SIR GALAHAD, A VERY PERFECT KNIGHT, AND THE MIRACLE OF THE GRAIL

After Merlin left, Arthur often sat and thought about the wizard's prophecies, especially one of them.

Merlin had said that when the most perfect knight arrives, it will mark the end of the Round Table, and the final days of the Kingdom of Logres.

One Whitsuntide, that prophecy came true. A strange pair appeared in Catmelot.

The handsome knight's fur was white as snow, and his blue eyes sparkled.

"This is Sir Galahad!" declared the old gentleman who accompanied him. "He comes to take his place at the Round Table."

And suddenly Galahad's name appeared on the back of the chair known as the Siege Perilous. Without hesitation, the knight sat himself down.

Not a hair on his tail was harmed.

The tomcat knights couldn't believe their eyes.

"But Merlin said the knight should be gold like the sun", grumbled Sir Kay, who remembered what happened to HIM on that chair. "He looks like any old cat to me."

"You foolish tom! He has a *heart* of gold", replied the bearded old gentleman angrily.

And then there was a clap of thunder,
and above the Round Table appeared
a glowing jug, richly decorated.
Into each cup was poured the most
delicious, thick dairy cream imaginable.

A deep booming voice rang out.

"Knights! This is the Dairy Grail,
a cream jug that is forever full, a miracle
among miracles! Let the most perfect
of all cats search and find it."

After one lick, the knights went
completely wild: "More, more!"
they cried.

But the cream jug had vanished.

Sir Gawain was the first to his feet.

"I shall search for that jug, and I shall
not return before I have licked it clean",
he declared.

"No! I shall be the one to find it",
shouted Sir Lancelot.

"Let us all ride at dawn in search of
this miracle", urged Sir Bors.

By sunrise all the knights were gone,
save Sir Kay, who preferred the idea
of loafing by the warm fireplace in
Catmelot.

"Is this what Merlin meant?" sighed
Arthur, looking at the empty table.

THE QUEST FOR THE GRAIL

The knights galloped north and south, east and west. They looked everywhere, but all in vain.
"WHERE IS THAT HOLY SUPERBOWL?"
they all asked.

The Castle of Pelles the Lame

The faraway city of Sarras

A barque

The Isle of Wonders

The Maidens' Convent

SIR MORDRED

Of course, in the end it was Sir Galahad who discovered the Grail.

But Galahad never returned to the Round Table. Many other knights fell by the wayside, too. After once tasting the Grail Cream, the Catmelot food held no attractions for them any longer.

There were new knights at the court now, younger cats. And then one day Sir Mordred arrived.

"Kaa-ak! I am the foundling child of Arthur and also Arthur's nephew", he squawked proudly.

Long ago, Arthur had found a fine dragon's egg and given it to one of his sisters. Unfortunately, the only thing that hatched out of the egg was this magpie, Mordred.

Arthur's sister had brought him up as a knight, and now Mordred had come to Catmelot.

Mordred was a sneaky chap, with a very high opinion of himself. He teased Arthur's older tomcats whenever he had the chance. And he found a partner in Gawain's brother Agravain, who was always looking to stir up trouble.

Like all magpies, Sir Mordred was very fond of jewels and anything that glittered, but when he saw King Arthur's sword and all the jewels in his crown, he went completely crazy.

"Kaa-ak! I want them, I *need* them", he chattered, and he began to hatch a plot to steal them.

Mordred heard a whisper that whenever Arthur was away, Guinevere was still using the Round Table for darts.

"Merlin's not here any more", said Guinevere when the loyal Sir Lancelot reminded her of the oath they had sworn.

Mordred naturally told Arthur everything.

"They must be punished according to the Laws of Logres!" tattled the magpie.

Arthur didn't think it was so important, but of course he remembered the promise made to Merlin.

"You'll have to prove it to me", he said, unable to think of any better answer.

Mordred had a plan ready.

"Pretend you are going on a hunting trip, Sire", said the magpie in a sneaky voice. "But as soon as you leave the castle, hide in a bush. I'll see to the rest."

Arthur had to agree to Mordred's scheme. He would have liked to warn Sir Lancelot, but there was no time.

Of course, Mordred was perfectly right.

As soon as the king had ridden out of the gates, Guinevere and her ladies-in-waiting carried the Round Table down to the cellar, and the darts competition began.

The game was in full swing when Mordred and his gang rushed into the cellar.

"It's a trap!" bellowed Lancelot.

There was a terrible kerfuffle after that. The table fell over, and Queen Guinevere and her supporters would have given Mordred and Agravain a real clobbering if Arthur had not appeared at the door. Lancelot hightailed it out of the window.

"Oh, what an awful business", Arthur moped to Sir Kay and Sir Gawain. "I shall have to punish Guinevere, and Lancelot, too, when he is caught. It is the law of the land – anyone who breaks their promise must be dipped in tar and rolled in feathers."

"How ghastly!" shuddered Gawain.

For cats, the very idea of tarring and feathering made their tails tremble. Feathers were for birds.

The only consolation was that Guinevere was only a dog after all, but it was still pretty awful.

But the law was the law, and not even the queen could be above the law.

"Sir Lancelot will find a way to help the queen, you mark my words", muttered Gawain to himself.

"Go on! Dunk the mangy mutt in the barrel!" screamed Sir Mordred, as Guinevere was brought into the square in chains.

"That's where you belong, you wormy apology for a bird!" barked Guinevere.

Arthur had ordered the Orkney brothers to be on the platform to make sure that the queen was not dipped too deeply into the tar barrel.

"Let the sentence be carried out!" said Arthur wearily.

But just then Lancelot galloped into the square and rescued the queen.

"Seize the traitor!" squawked Mordred, flapping his wings.

But they were no match for a knight like Sir Lancelot. Lancelot took Guinevere to safety at his own castle.

In all the chaos that went on, Agravain accidentally tipped the tar barrel over Sir Gawain, and poor Gawain toppled into the basket of feathers.

"Lancelot did it!" lied Mordred. "I saw him!"

Sir Gawain was furious. He picked feathers from his tar-covered coat. "That Lancelot is no friend of mine now!"

Many of the Knights of the Round Table left Arthur to join Lancelot.

Mordred rubbed his feathers in delight.

"The crown and the sword will soon be mine", he squawked.

"Go get your queen back and show who is High King here", Mordred screeched in Arthur's ears.

Gawain agreed: "That frog-faced Lancelot has to be tarred and feathered, *and* feathered and tarred!" he thundered, even though he and Lancelot were old friends.

"Oh, dear! Very well, let's go then!" agreed Arthur at last.

The cats didn't feel like fighting against their friends, however, so what happened was that Arthur's army sat outside Lancelot's castle, with Lancelot's troops inside.

Sir Gawain was the only one who howled and growled and jumped up and down by the walls.

Arthur had left the magpie Sir Mordred in charge of Catmelot
while he was away. The other knights couldn't understand this.
Naturally, Mordred's ally Agravain had stayed behind to
help the bird.

"Just leave your crown and your sword
with me. You don't want to get
them all dusty and scratched
on the battlefield, do you now?"
Mordred had said.
"And you *know* you can
trust me, after all I'm
almost your own son!"

"You can guard my crown, but I'm not leaving
Excalibur", Arthur had replied. "And remember,
nobody is to touch my crown. No, not even you!"

Of course, as soon as Arthur was out of sight,
the sneaky Mordred put on the king's royal
robes and crown, and plumped himself on
the throne.
"I have the crown, and I shall soon
have that sword. You'll see", he
cawed smugly to Agravain.

That night, Mordred and
Agravain hid the Round
Table in the highest tower
in the castle. In the morning,
they called the castle staff
together in the courtyard.

"Kaaa-akk! King Arthur
has joined Lancelot's band
of thugs!" Mordred wailed.
"He has stolen the Round
Table and taken it to
Lancelot's castle as a dart-
board. Any cat who defies
Merlin's sacred oath no
longer deserves to be
King!" he screamed.
   "The crown belongs to
me, an honest magpie!"

Agravain did his best, too:
"Long live the new King of
the Cats, long live Mordred!"
he shouted.

The castle staff didn't know what to think.
Was a magpie really now King of the Cats?

"But Mordred, what do we do when Arthur gets back?"
whispered a worried Agravain.
   "We invite the seawolves, the beach-rats, and
      all the lowlife of Logres to join us", explained
         the magpie, his eyes gleaming. "We put
            together a massive army, and then we
               swipe that gleaming sword right
                  out of Arthur's hands!"

"And then as High King of Logres I shall collect all the jewels and pretty bangles in the realm, for nobody in Logres shall be allowed to look as fine as me, King Mordred!"

It was a great plan, but unfortunately the cats patched up their quarrel.

Guinevere promised that she would now keep her promises.

Arthur promised that the Queen wouldn't be punished, and Lancelot promised to make Guinevere a proper dartboard, and also that he would clean up Sir Gawain's coat.

Mordred had gone off to gather his troops when Arthur rode into Catmelot and heard what had happened.

"That scheming popinjay has gone and pinched my crown, has he?" growled Arthur, and he and his knights galloped after Mordred.

THE LAST GREAT BATTLE

Arthur's troops searched high and low for Mordred.

At last, one evening at sunset, they met the rebels.

Arthur was shocked at the size of the army Mordred had put together, many times larger than his own. Half of Arthur's knights had stayed behind at Sir Lancelot's castle.

"What are we to do against those thugs and villains?" said Gawain, who had gone very pale.

Fortunately, darkness fell before either side could get any further than shouting insults at each other. Everyone settled down for a good night's sleep.

During the night, Arthur had a strange dream: Merlin and Nimue appeared in his tent.

"Delay the battle for as long as you can", advised Merlin. "I shall send Lancelot to help you. Mordred will turn and run when he sees you two both against him. You'll get your crown back."

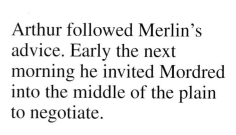

Arthur followed Merlin's advice. Early the next morning he invited Mordred into the middle of the plain to negotiate.

Both sides were very wary of the meeting.

Mordred agreed to a truce on condition that he would have the crown, Excalibur, Catmelot, and the Kingdom of Logres. Arthur would be allowed to keep Tintagel Castle.

"That sounds alright", bluffed Arthur. "Could I have a day or two to think it over?"

But then disaster struck. An ugly snake slithered out of a hole and bit Agravain on the back of his paw.

"OWW!" cried the tomcat, and pulled out his sword.

In the wink of an eye, all the swords were bared on both sides.

"Look out! I don't want scratches on Excalibur", cried Mordred.

But it was too late.

The fight was on.

The noise was deafening. The thunder of battle carried far and wide, even to Lancelot and his knights as they galloped southwards. They were coming, but they arrived too late.

It was the battle to end all battles, a fight of the kind that had never been witnessed before in cat history, and would never be seen again.

By evening there wasn't anyone left on either side to raise a paw in anger.

"Hooo-W-who won?" croaked Arthur.
   But nobody knew.
   At that moment, a black, dust-covered bird fluttered unsteadily into the air by his ear.
   "MORDRED!" roared Arthur, and with his final ounce of strength he slashed at the magpie with a flagstaff.

Mordred went "Kaaa-akk!" and flopped down on Arthur's head.
   Arthur fell into a deep sleep.
   (Nobody ever heard anything from Mordred after that.)
   Long afterwards tales were told of the great battle of Camlann Plain, for Camlann was the name of the place.

SIR BEDIVERE AND EXCALIBUR

Sir Bedivere gently woke the king.

Arthur sighed: "The story of Logres is at an end", he said sadly. "But there is still one job to do. Bedivere, my friend, take Excalibur, and cast it back to the Lake of Reeds."

Sir Bedivere took the sword, and walked to the water.

"It seems a shame to throw away such a fine sword", he thought, and he hid Excalibur in the reeds.

"What did you see...?" enquired Arthur. "What did you see when the sword fell into the lake?"

"A big splash, Sire", replied the knight.

"Then you did not do as I ordered", said the king. "Now get moving and throw Excalibur into the lake!"

Bedivere went once more, but again he could not give up the sword.

"Now what did you see?" asked Arthur.

"A b-bigger splash this time", stuttered the knight.

Bedivere had to go back a third time.

And now the sword flew through the air towards the lake.

Just as it was coming down, a hand appeared from the water and caught the sword. The only sound was a gentle swish, as Excalibur sank beneath the surface.

"The Maiden of the Lake has received her own back", said Arthur, when Bedivere told him what he had seen.

From across the lake a black barge drifted into view.
  "It is the boat come to carry me to Avalon", said Arthur.
"The maidens have been sent to fetch me home."
  And to the sounds of beautiful music and song, the boat
carried the greatest of all the kings of the cats towards
the island looming up out of the mist, to Avalon under the
apple trees, to the place they call the Isle of Glass.

"We'll follow you, my Lord, even if we have to swim
over!" called Gawain, as the king departed.

AVALON

The time of the cats in the Kingdom of Logres was at an end.
But in Avalon, the party was in full swing. One by one, all
the ladies of Catmelot and the Knights of the Round Table
arrived, and if you listen very hard, you can probably still
hear their merry-making to this day.

Now all this happened a very long time ago, long before humans came along.

But there are still some signs to be seen of the heroic times of the cats. Probably the most famous, and certainly the largest, are one or two mysterious giant figures drawn on chalk hillsides. Sadly, these, too, have changed over the centuries and some have even grassed over.

Amongst the alley cats there is also a persistent rumour that the Round Table still exists, that Arthur's shield and his helmet have been found from the bottom of the river, and that they are now on show in a museum somewhere. Who knows?

(Of course dogs say that the cats are just bragging, but then they *would* say that, wouldn't they?)